THIS **ELEPHANT & PIGGIE** BOOK
BELONGS TO:

_____

_____

_____

To Lowell, Lee and Chelsea

# I Love My New Toy!

By **Mo Willems**

**WALKER BOOKS**
AND SUBSIDIARIES
LONDON · BOSTON · SYDNEY · AUCKLAND

An **ELEPHANT & PIGGIE** Book

I love
throwing toys.

Yes!

Zip!

Thanks.

Turn

16

Here it comes!

ZOOM!

I broke your toy.

You broke my toy.

And sad.

26

I am sorry.

32

No!
My new toy
is broken!

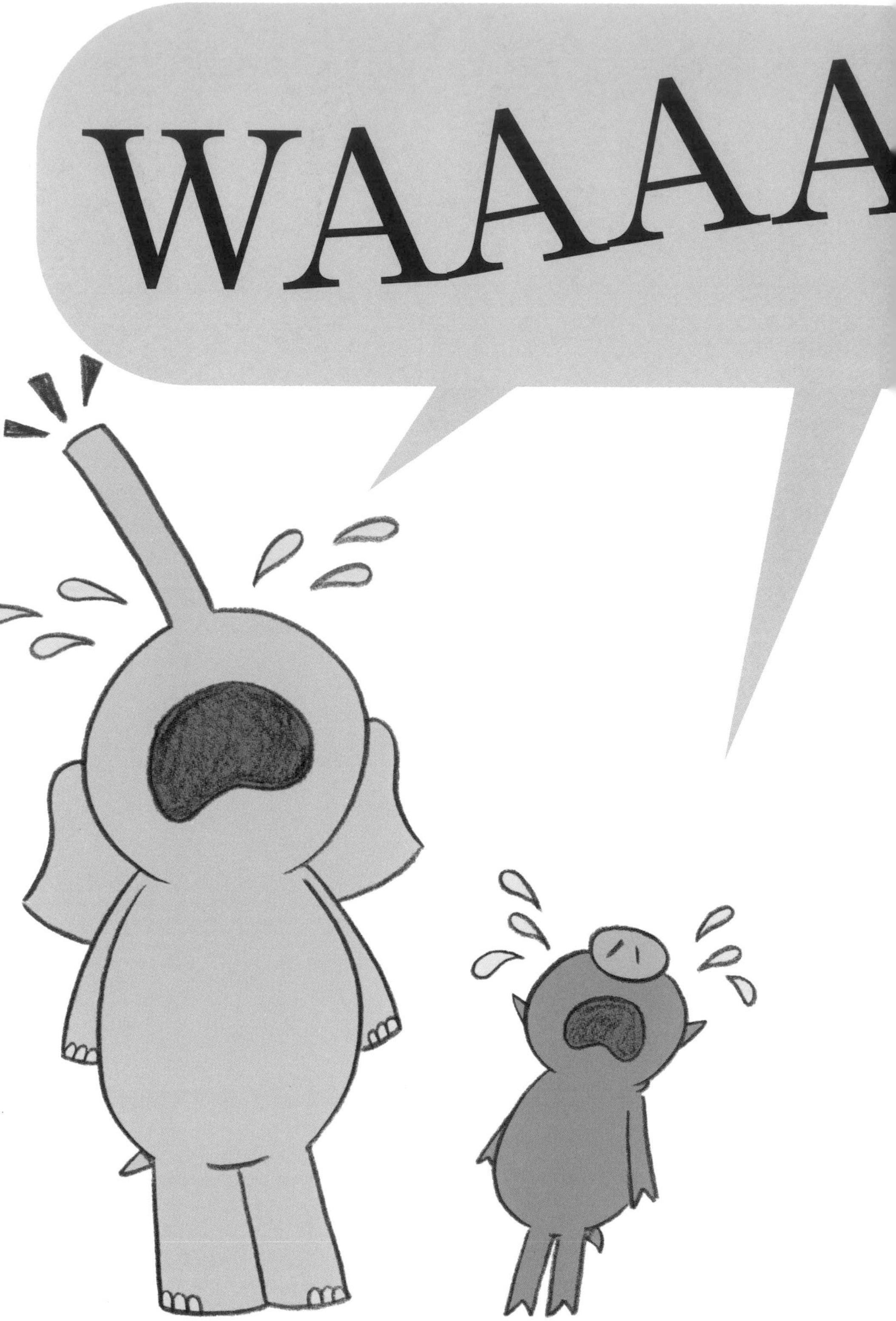
WAAAA

AAAAA!

AAAAA!

Cool!

You have a
break-and-snap
toy.

SNAP!

Enjoy!

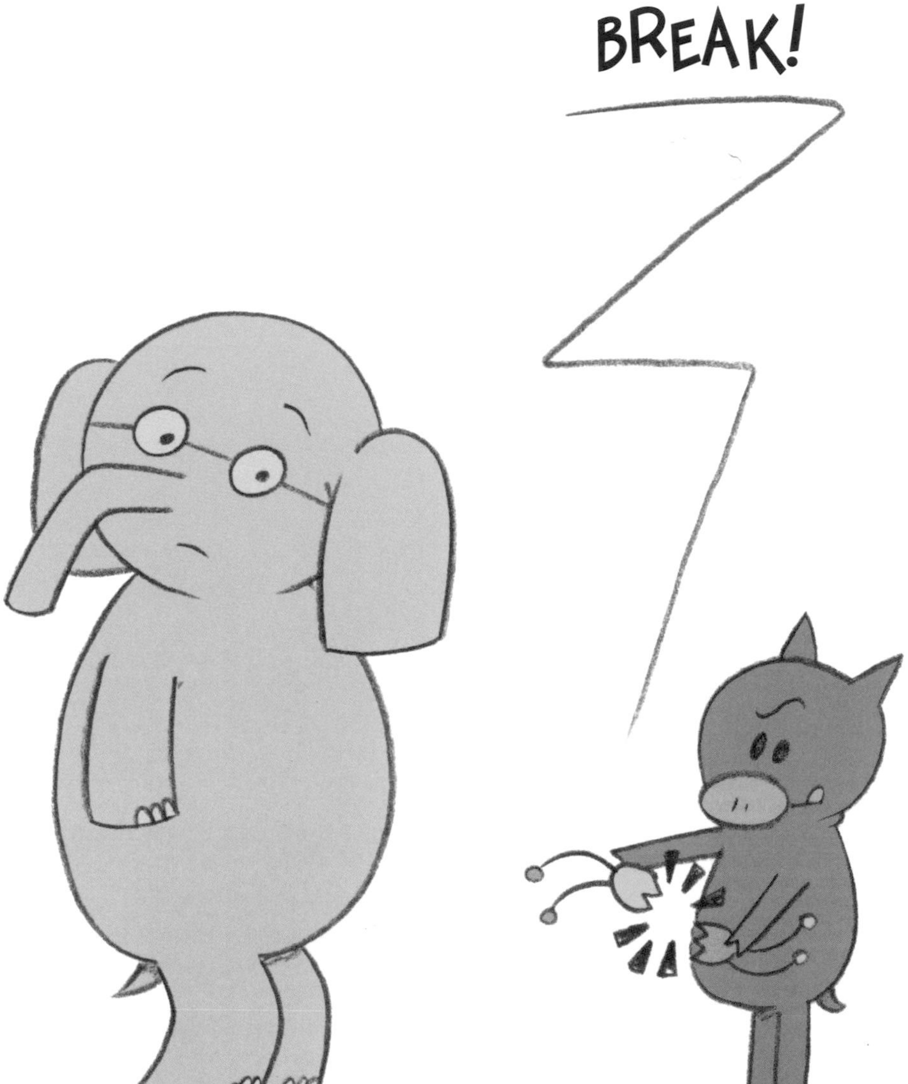
BREAK!

SNAP!

BREAK!

SNAP!

# No.

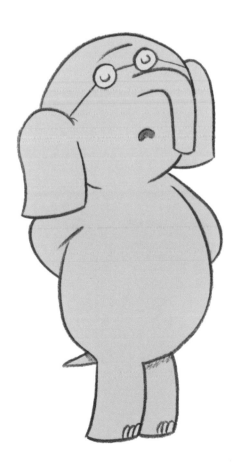

You do not want to play
with my new toy?

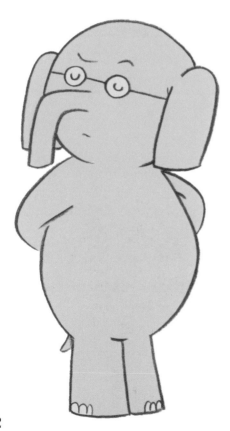

I do not want to play
with your new toy.

# I want to play with you.

# Friends are more fun than toys.

Mo Willems is the author of the Caldecott Honor-winning books
*Knuffle Bunny: A Cautionary Tale* and *Don't Let the Pigeon Drive the Bus!*
His other groundbreaking books include *Leonardo, the Terrible Monster*; *Edwina, the
Dinosaur Who Didn't Know She was Extinct* and *There Is a Bird on Your Head!*,
which won the American Library Association's 2008 Theodor Seuss Geisel Award
for the most distinguished book for beginner readers.

Mo began his career as a writer and animator on *Sesame Street*,
where he garnered six Emmy Awards.

First published in Great Britain 2008 by Walker Books Ltd
87 Vauxhall Walk, London SE11 5HJ

2 4 6 8 10 9 7 5 3 1

First published in the United States by Hyperion Books for Children.
British publication rights arranged with Sheldon Fogelman Agency, Inc.

The right of Mo Willems to be identified as author and illustrator of this work has been
asserted by him in accordance with the Copyright, Designs and Patents Act 1988

This book has been typeset in Century 725 and Grilled Cheese

Printed in Singapore

British Library Cataloguing in Publication Data:
a catalogue record for this book is available from the British Library

ISBN 978-1-4063-1471-7

www.walkerbooks.co.uk

www.pigeonpresents.com